Tucking Mommy In

by Morag Loh

illustrated by
Donna Rawlins

ORCHARD BOOKS

New York

Tucking Mommy In

◆ ◆ ◆

For Su-lin, Mei-lin,
and for Donna's family

Text copyright © 1987 by Morag Loh
Illustrations copyright © 1987 by Donna Rawlins
Originally published in Australia by Ashton Scholastic
First American hardcover edition 1988 published by Orchard Books
First paperback edition 1991
Orchard Books
A division of Franklin Watts, Inc.
387 Park Avenue South
New York, New York 10016
The text of this book is set in 18 point Bembo.
The illustrations are watercolor and colored pencil.
Printed and bound in the United States of America
Book design by Sylvia Frezzolini

10 9 8 7 6 5 4 3 2 1

Library of Congress Cataloging-in-Publication Data
Loh, Morag Jeannette, 1935-   Tucking Mommy in / by Morag Loh:
illustrated by Donna Rawlins. p.   cm.   Summary: Two sisters tuck their
mother into bed one evening when she is especially tired.
ISBN 0-531-05740-2.   ISBN 0-531-08340-3 (lib. bdg.)
ISBN 0-531-07025-5 (pbk.)
[1. Sisters—Fiction.   2. Mothers and daughters—Fiction.   3. Bedtime—
Fiction.] I. Rawlins, Donna, ill.   II. Title. PZ7.L8289Tu   1988
[E]-dc19   87-16740   CIP   AC

"As soon as I've tucked you two in," Mommy said,
"I'm going to bed myself. I'm so tired that I can't
think straight."

"Let me tell the bedtime story tonight," said Sue.
"Then you won't have to think at all."
"That sounds great," said Mommy.

But Jenny wasn't so sure.
"I hope you can tell a good story, Sue," she said.

Mommy kissed them both and tucked them in.

Then she lay down on Jenny's bed.
Sue made up a story about their cat, Mitzi.

The story was funny and Jenny asked many questions.

But Mommy didn't say anything.
"Mommy's asleep!" Jenny said.

"What do we do now?" asked Sue.

Jenny shook Mommy gently,
but Mommy kept on sleeping.

Sue came over to Jenny's bed.
"Wake up, Mommy!"

"Mmmm," said Mommy, but she did not wake up.
"We'll have to do something else," said Sue.

They shook Mommy quite hard.
"You can't go to sleep
with all your clothes on," said Sue.

Mommy opened her eyes and struggled to sit up.
"I'm sorry, kids," she said.
"I didn't mean to go to sleep."

"You'd better go to bed right now," said Sue.
"We'll tuck ourselves in tonight."

"Thank you darlings," said Mommy.

Sue and Jenny led her to her bedroom.

They helped her undress and put on her pajamas.

Then they tucked her into bed and gave her a kiss.
Mommy smiled sleepily.

"Tell the story about Mitzi again, Sue," said Jenny.
By the time Sue was finished, Mommy was fast asleep.

When Daddy came home from work,
Sue and Jenny ran to meet him.
They told him all about tucking Mommy in.

"Mommy *must* have been tired," he said.

"Would you like me to tell you a story now?" Daddy asked.

"No thanks," said Jenny.
"Sue told a good story—twice—and I'm sleepy."

Sue yawned. "Me too," she said.
Daddy tucked them in.

"Thanks for taking such good care of Mommy,"
Daddy said. He put out the light.
"See you in the morning."